Pod

Trixie

Pod loves to build
things out of the
bits and bobs he
finds. He also loves
his tutu!

Yawn! When
she's not dancing,
Trixie likes curling
up and having
a nice snooze.

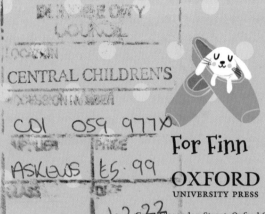

For Finn

OXFORD
UNIVERSITY PRESS

Great Clarendon Street, Oxford OX2 6DP
Oxford University Press is a department of the University of Oxford.
It furthers the University's objective of excellence in research, scholarship,
and education by publishing worldwide. Oxford is a registered trade mark
of Oxford University Press in the UK and in certain other countries

Text copyright © Swapna Reddy 2022
Illustrations copyright © Binny Talib 2022

The moral rights of the author/illustrator have been asserted

Database right Oxford University Press (maker)

First published 2022

British Library Cataloguing in Publication Data

Data available

ISBN: 978-0-19-277490-3

1 3 5 7 9 10 8 6 4 2

Printed in China

Paper used in the production of this book is a natural,
recyclable product made from wood grown in sustainable forests.
The manufacturing process conforms to the environmental
regulations of the country of origin.

Ballet Bunnies

Trixie is Missing

By Swapna Reddy

Illustrated by Binny Talib

OXFORD
UNIVERSITY PRESS

Chapter 1

'Come on, Mum,' Millie
squealed with excitement.

It was the morning of the dress
rehearsal for Miss Luisa's School of
Dance showcase at the Town Hall. Since
the rehearsal didn't start until later that
afternoon, Mum had promised Millie that

they would go for a hot chocolate at their
favourite café once they had picked up
Millie's costume and sequins for the show.

But first, Millie had to pick up four
very important guests for their day out.
Four very important Ballet Bunny guests.

'I'm coming,' Mum laughed as she
hurried down the stairs to the landing
where a very excited and quite impatient
Millie was waiting.

Mum grabbed Millie's hand, spun
her around, and they danced out of the doorway.

They skipped all the way up the road
and straight through the doors of the
dance school. Mum went to find Miss
Luisa to pick up Millie's costume, and
Millie took her chance to sneak into the
studio. This was the studio where Millie
had first met the little Ballet Bunnies,
who had since become firm friends.
There she found Fifi, Dolly, Pod, and a
very sleepy Trixie waiting at the edge of
the stage for her. All four bunnies jumped
with excitement, their long, silky ears
flopping about as they spotted Millie.

'Oh, bunny fluff!' Fifi exclaimed.
'I do love a day out.'

'Mum promised hot chocolates once we've picked up sequins for my costume,' Millie grinned.

'It's not a day out without hot chocolate,' Dolly sang as she pirouetted around Millie's bag.

Millie scooped up the bunnies into a ginormous cuddle, then set them back down on the stage by her bag. Dolly looped paws with Fifi and twirled her around as she sang out her chocolate song.

'Hot chocolate, hot chocolate,
Oh, it's not a day out without
hot chocolate!

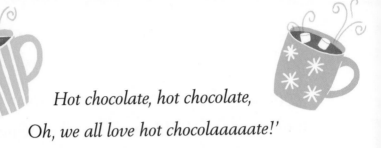

Hot chocolate, hot chocolate,
Oh, we all love hot chocolaaaaate!'

Millie giggled as the Fifi joined in
with Dolly's hot chocolate song and the
two bunnies hopped into her rucksack.

'All aboard!' Pod announced as
he climbed up Millie's arm, along her
shoulder, to take a seat in the hood of
her jacket.

'You're wearing your lucky hairclip,'
Pod said, spotting the fluffy clip the
bunnies had gifted Millie at the start of
her dance lessons.

'It's my favourite,' Millie said, gently

tapping the hair slide. 'Whenever I wear
it on stage, it feels like you are all dancing
with me.'

She patted Pod on his head as he
nestled in the place and reached down
towards the smallest of the bunnies.

'And where would you like to sit
today?' Millie asked Trixie, who yawned
so loudly that she almost got Millie
yawning too.

'I'm so tired today, Millie,' Trixie said, stifling another yawn. Her eyelids drooped shut as Millie stroked her soft, grey fur. 'Can I go somewhere cosy where I can take a long nap?'

'I know just the place,' Millie said and she placed Trixie in the fleece-lined pocket of her bag.

Millie held a finger up to her lips so the other bunnies knew not to wake Trixie. They all quickly ducked out of sight as the studio door swung open.

'Come on, Millie,' Mum squealed with excitement.

'I'm coming,' Millie laughed, as she hurried out of the studio.

Chapter 2

The next stop for Mum and Millie
was the Costume Shop. It was the best
place for sequins and it was one of their
favourite stores. The shop was packed
full of fabrics and hats and costumes
on long racks that stretched the entire
length of the store.

Mum and Millie headed straight
for the huge fluffy feathers by the bead
display. They threw on matching feather
boas and floppy hats before striking poses
in front of the store mirror.

'Oh, Millie,' Mum laughed as Millie piled on hat after hat after hat until she was mainly just a stack of hats.

As Millie tidied, Mum went off to find sequins for Millie's tutu. Once she had finished, and seeing Mum was still busy, Millie and the bunnies headed to the back of the store.

'Look at all these ribbons,' Dolly squealed, jumping out of Millie's bag.

The back wall of the shop, draped in satin ribbons of every colour, reminded Millie of a rainbow after a downpour. Dolly leapt onto the countertop by the wall and grabbed the end of a purple ribbon, wrapping it around her waist.

Pod hopped to the other side of the wall and tied the end of a green ribbon to his paw. Fifi didn't want to miss out on the fun so she jumped over too and pulled down the end of the yellow ribbon and the three bunnies danced in and out and

over and under, creating their very
own maypole.

'I could spend all day here,' Dolly
said. She hopped over to the nearby
shelf and bounced into the stacks of
tutus, disappearing into the soft folds of
shimmery tulle.

'But what about our hot chocolates?'
Millie asked.

'Oh, bunny fluff!' Dolly cried.
Nothing in the world could keep a bunny
away from their hot chocolate. 'Let's go!'
she said, pulling Pod and Fifi after her.

The bunnies hopped back into
Millie's bag and Millie followed Mum out
of the Costume Shop to the café.

⊙ ✳ ⊙

The café was right by the town's
theatre, and its walls were covered in
pictures of dancers and musicians.
Millie loved looking at all of
the drawings and paintings.

Mum went to the counter and ordered hot chocolates for them both, whilst Millie showed the bunnies her favourite pictures on the wall.

'It just looks like a swirl of white paint,' Pod said as Millie pointed to a painting.

'It's a dancer,' Millie replied. 'A
ballerina who has been caught in the
middle of a pirouette.'

'You're right!' Fifi said, tilting her
head. 'I see her now!'

Mum was heading back to the table with the hot chocolates, so Millie quickly went over and took a seat. When Mum went to get napkins, Millie carefully tipped out a little of her drink into her saucer for the bunnies and placed it on the chair next to her. She tucked the chair in tight so Mum wouldn't spot the bunnies lapping up the hot chocolate.

'Mmmm,' Dolly said, her whiskers dripping with chocolate. 'Delicious!'

'What was that?' Mum asked, sitting down.

Millie froze, sure that Mum had discovered the bunnies.

But just as she opened her mouth to try and explain the talking bunnies hiding under the table and drinking some of her hot chocolate out of a saucer, the door to the café swung open.

'Millie!' a voice called.

It was Samira, Millie's best friend from ballet class.

'We are going to the park before rehearsal,' Samira said. 'Do you want to come?'

Millie looked at Mum and nodded eagerly.

'Sure.' Mum smiled. 'Let's get these hot chocolates to go!'

Chapter 3

Millie and Samira skipped all the way from the park to the Town Hall. Their cheeks flushed red from running up and down the slide the wrong way, and seeing who could reach the furthest part of the sky on the swings. They chattered excitedly about the show nonstop.

The Ballet Bunnies stayed out of sight at the park, playing nearby in the long grass. They ran up and down a tree stump and then hopped as high as they could to see who could reach as far as Millie on the swings.

The bunnies even joined in from afar when Millie and Samira practised their steps in the park ahead of the big rehearsal, before following Millie, Samira, and the mums all the way to the Town Hall.

At rehearsal, Millie and Samira's mums waved off the girls and took a seat with the other parents. Millie and Samira joined the rest of their class as Miss Luisa talked to the students.

Once it was time to take to the stage, Millie trailed behind her class at a safe distance where she could talk to the Ballet Bunnies without anyone seeing.

'Good luck, Millie,' Dolly whispered as Fifi and Pod gathered in close for a hug.

Millie grinned at the bunnies. She had been part of a few performances now and still felt nervous. But having the

Ballet Bunnies there made the nerves feel a little less each time.

As the music played, Millie and her class danced the steps they had been taught. All the practising made Millie feel very confident. She kept her chin up and didn't have to look down at her feet once.

Out of the corner of her eye, she could see the other dancers moving in perfect time with her and Millie couldn't stop smiling.

'Lovely work, everyone,' Miss Luisa praised. 'All your hard work is paying off.'

The next part of the routine involved retracing their dance steps back to where they had started. Millie had always found this a bit tricky, but she took a breath, focussed, and found she didn't miss a step.

'Well done, Millie,' Miss Luisa said at the end of rehearsal. 'That was your best performance yet.'

Millie felt so proud.

Chapter 4

'Make sure you have all your bits and bobs before you leave, children,' Miss Luisa called out. 'Tomorrow is the big show!'

As the children took their costumes and said goodbye to one another, Millie found herself alone at the side of the stage. She collected up her costume and jacket and packed up her bag.

'My lucky hair clip!' she exclaimed,
patting her hair.

'What's wrong, Millie?' Fifi asked,
hopping over with Dolly and Pod.

'I can't find my hair clip,' Millie said.

She emptied her rucksack and carefully sifted through her belongings. There was her hairbrush, her hair ties, her spare tights, and her water bottle. But no hair clip.

'It must have fallen somewhere,' Dolly said. 'We'll help you find it.'

The bunnies hopped off in different directions as Millie searched her bag and costume again.

Dolly rifled under the props on the stage. But there was no lucky hair clip there.

Pod rummaged at the side of the stage. He found an abandoned sock and three hair grips but no lucky hair clip.

Fifi looked at the front of the stage.
She searched amongst the lights and the rails
but didn't find the lucky hair clip either.

All three bunnies rushed back to
Millie's side.

'I don't know where it is,' Millie said tearfully. She couldn't bear to search her bag another time, but she didn't know where else to look.

'Don't worry, Millie,' Pod reassured her. 'Four sets of eyes are better than one and five sets of eyes are even better than four.'

'By bunny fluff,' Fifi said. 'You're right, Pod! Let's wake up Trixie and get an extra set of eyes to help.'

The bunnies jumped over to Millie's bag where Dolly carefully pushed open the zipper and burrowed inside.

'Trixie?' she called gently, hoping not to wake the little bunny with too much of a start.

She peered in the bag further before whipping round to face the others.

As she looked at Millie, Fifi, and Pod, her face paled and her eyes grew wide with shock.

'Oh, bunny fluff,' Dolly gasped. 'Trixie's missing too!'

Chapter 5

'Millie, what's wrong?' Mum asked, as she spotted Millie frantically searching her bag again.

The bunnies hopped out of sight as quick as a flash.

'I can't find Trixie!' Millie blurted out.

'Who's Trixie?' Mum replied, confused.

Millie gulped. She'd completely forgotten only she knew about the Ballet Bunnies.

'Trixie is my . . . my . . .' Millie
stammered. 'My lucky hairclip,' she
added quickly.

'Oh Millie,' Mum said, scooping her
up in a big cuddle.

'I can't do the show without her,' Millie cried. 'I mean 'it'. I can't do the show without it.'

'Have you had a good look around?' Mum asked.

'I have. I've looked everywhere. It's completely lost,' Millie said, tears starting to roll down her cheeks. 'It's all my fault.'

Mum wiped away the tears from Millie's cheeks and smoothed back her hair. 'Sometimes things get misplaced but it's OK,' Mum said. 'It's no one's fault.'

Mum checked the stage, the props, and rummaged through the piles of costumes. She looked up and down the corridor

and had a look in Millie's bag too, but she couldn't find Millie's lucky hairclip either. She tidied up Millie's belongings back into her bag as Millie copied Mum, searching the stage, the corridor, and the costumes. 'Perhaps you dropped it on your way here,' Mum suggested to Millie.

Millie couldn't focus on Mum's words. Her mind whirred. She felt frightened at the thought of Trixie being somewhere unfamiliar all alone.

Mum took Millie's hands in hers, bringing Millie's worried mind back to where they were. 'When I misplace things, I find retracing my steps helps,'

Mum said.

'Retracing your steps?' Millie
repeated back.

'Yes,' Mum nodded. 'I think about
where I have been and I follow my steps
back.'

'Like in the dance routine?' Millie
asked, confused.

'Exactly!' Mum said. 'Your hairclip
is clearly not here and you definitely
had it when we left home this morning.'
She pulled Millie to her feet and swung
Millie's bag over her shoulder. 'If we
follow our steps back to where we were
last, we might find it along the way.'

She hugged Millie close. 'We'll retrace
our steps just like in your dance routine.
Don't worry, Millie.'

Chapter 6

'Where do we need to go first?' Mum asked.

Millie thought hard. 'We need to go to the park!' she cried. *That was the last place they were before they got to the Town Hall!*

'Well remembered, Millie,' Mum said.

She pushed Mum ahead of her, giving Dolly, Pod, and Fifi a chance to clamber into her bag and out of sight.

'Let's go!' the bunnies urged Millie who needed no encouragement at all. She had to find Trixie.

In the corridor, Millie ran fast, pulling hard on Mum's hand and dragging her out of the front doors towards the park.

'Slow down, Millie,' Mum said. 'We might miss something.'

Millie stopped and looked around her feet.

'We have to retrace our steps just like in the dance routine, remember?' Mum explained. 'Let's carefully look along the route we took.'

Millie glanced up and down the pavement. She thought back to her and Samira skipping along the way earlier that day. She didn't recognize the green bin or the red post box. *Of course! They hadn't come that way at all!* That's why it looked unfamiliar. They had *crossed* the road in front of the Town Hall.

'We need to cross back across the road,' she exclaimed.

'That's right, Millie,' Mum said.

Millie crossed the road with Mum, keeping an eye on traffic, whilst Mum also looked around their feet for the lost hairclip.

Once they were safely across, Millie
and Mum followed their steps back
towards the park—Mum combing the
pavement for the lucky hair clip and
Millie searching for little Trixie.

They followed their steps back towards where Millie and Samira had practised their dance. They followed their steps back to the swings and then to the slide where Millie had run up and down the wrong way. They followed their steps back towards the entrance of the park by the café.

But there was no sign of Trixie anywhere.

'Not here,' Millie said to Mum, her voice small and quivering.

'Don't worry,' Mum reassured. 'Let's just keep following our steps back.'

Millie nodded and they went to the café.

Millie remembered exactly where she and the bunnies had had their hot chocolates.

She was about to rush over when she remembered she needed to follow her steps back in the right order. So, she carefully passed the paintings she had seen that morning and then checked under the tables and chairs before arriving back at the table they had sat at.

But Trixie was nowhere to be seen.

Chapter 7

Millie's mind reeled with fear. What if Trixie was lost? What if she was all alone and frightened?

Mum asked the waitress if she had seen a lucky hair clip but the waitress had not. Mum saw Millie's face fall at the news and she saw Millie's eyes well with

tears again.

'Don't worry, Millie,' Mum soothed.
She held up her small shopping bag full
of sequins. 'We still have one more place
to follow our steps back to.'

The Costume Shop!

Millie and Mum thanked the waitress and then hurried out of the café, almost tripping over the steps.

They followed the route they had taken earlier, all the way back to the

Costume Shop. Along the way, Millie
searched the pavement. She worried that
Trixie had fallen from her pocket and
hurt herself.

But there was still no sign of Trixie
along the way.

When Millie and Mum arrived at the Costume Shop, Mum talked to the owner and asked if they had had any lost property handed in. Millie retraced her steps back to the ribbon wall where the bunnies had danced their maypole dance.

As Millie made her way towards the hat stand, a sound caught her ear. She stopped and listened hard.

There it was again!

It was a quiet hum, like the gentle buzz of a little snore.

Millie shut her eyes so she could concentrate on the sound.

This time she was sure of what she

was hearing.

It was the sound of a sleeping
Ballet Bunny.

Tucked up in the soft felt of an
upturned cowboy hat was a little grey
Ballet Bunny, fast asleep with her paws
wrapped around a very lucky hairclip.

Millie had found Trixie.

Chapter 8

Millie almost screamed with glee at the sight of Trixie balled up, fast asleep. But she knew better than to cause a commotion and have Mum running to the scene. And she definitely knew better than to startle a sleeping bunny awake.

Millie gently reached into the hat and

gave Trixie a stroke.

'Trixie?' Millie said gently. 'It's time to wake up.'

Trixie yawned and stretched out her legs. 'Millie!' she exclaimed. 'Where are the others?'

In Millie's relief, she couldn't help the tears that rolled down her face. It had been quite the day.

'Trixie! I've been looking for you everywhere!' she said.

Trixie could see how upset Millie was. 'Oh bunny fluff. I'm so sorry, Millie,' she said quietly.

'Where have you been?' Millie asked, wiping at her tears with her sleeve.

'I've been here the whole day,' Trixie explained. 'When we got to the shop this morning, I heard the others dancing by the ribbons and I woke up. I got out of my cosy pocket and decided to explore the shop. But when I came back, you were all gone.' The little bunny stared down at her paws. 'I should've told you I was exploring. I'm very sorry, Millie.' Trixie looked up at Millie. The tiny bunny did look very sorry indeed. 'I knew I should stay put in case you came back to look for me,' Trixie continued. 'And you did!'

Millie smiled. 'That was the right thing to do, Trixie.'

'Trixie!' Fifi exclaimed as she, Dolly, and Pod hopped out of Millie's bag to the familiar sound of Trixie's voice. 'We were so worried about you.'

'Trixie, you mustn't go off like that,' Dolly scolded her. She then gave her a big hug. 'I'm so glad Millie found you.'

'Me too,' Trixie smiled.

Millie and Pod told Trixie all about how they had searched the Town Hall after rehearsal and how Millie and Mum had followed their steps back to the Costume Shop. 'I was so scared when I couldn't find you. I thought you were sleeping in my bag,' Millie said.

'Well, I was asleep,' Trixie said. 'It just wasn't in your bag!'

Millie stroked Trixie's long silky ears and nuzzled in close. 'I'm very glad you're safe.'

Trixie grinned and hopped over to the hat to fetch Millie's hair clip.

'Where did you find this?' Millie exclaimed.

'It was in a stack of hats,' Trixie said. 'I thought it looked like yours so I held on to it for you.'

'Thank you, Trixie,' Millie said, fixing the clip back in her hair. She gathered up the bunnies. 'I think it's time we got you back in my bag.'

She tucked Trixie back into the cosy pocket of her bag as Dolly, Fifi, and Pod climbed into Millie's pockets and hood. The five friends headed back to the front of the store where Millie found Mum.

'I can't believe you found your

lucky hairclip, Millie!' Mum said, giving her
a big hug. 'It certainly is a lucky clip.'

And Millie couldn't have agreed more.

Chapter 9

Millie and the bunnies

couldn't wait for the show the next day.
They had gone straight home to Millie's
house from the Costume Shop. And at
home, Millie, Dolly, Fifi, and Pod had
been sure not to let Trixie out of their
sight for one moment.

The next morning, the bunnies
helped Millie practise her routine ahead
of the show. They had been a great help

and Millie couldn't wait to perform
the dance onstage with her class.

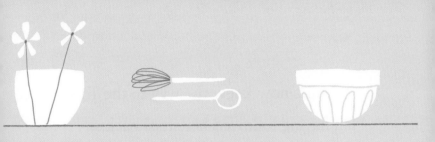

Millie now knew the way to the Town Hall having followed her steps back so precisely the previous day, so she led the way with the bunnies safely tucked away in her bag and Mum close behind.

Mum kissed Millie and wished her good luck at the side of the stage before joining the other parents in the audience and as soon as she had gone, Miss Luisa called all the children to the stage.

'It's time for you to dance,' Pod said to Millie.

Millie pinned her lucky hairclip on to her costume then she hugged each of the bunnies and ushered them off so they

could find a good spot in the audience to watch.

'Good luck,' Trixie whispered to Millie, before she headed off with the others.

It was Millie's big moment. She took a breath and stepped out onto the stage with her class. The music started, and the lights brightened. Millie held her head high, confident, and proud. She never missed a beat. She couldn't believe how far her dancing had come since her

very first lesson at Miss Luisa's School
of Dance. Her chest swelled with pride.
On stage, she looked and felt like a real
dancer.

But she couldn't have done it by
herself.

She spotted Mum whooping and
cheering her on from the audience. And
then Millie spotted four more familiar
faces in the crowd. Four familiar bunnies.

Millie's smile stretched from ear to
ear as she took a curtesy and she saw the
bunnies cheer for her from the audience.
And then she saw the bunnies pirouette
in perfect time with one another and *jeté*

off towards the side of the stage, ready
and waiting with a big bunny hug for her.
Because, after all, how else would good
friends end a wonderful ballet day?

Basic ballet moves

First position

Second position

Third
position

Fourth
position

Fifth position

About the author

Award-winning author Swapna Reddy, who also writes as Swapna Haddow, lives in New Zealand with her husband and son and their dog, Archie.

If she wasn't writing books, she would love to run a detective agency or wash windows because she's very nosy.

About the illustrator

Binny Talib is a Sydney based illustrator who loves to create wallpaper, branding, children's books, editorial, packaging and anything else she can draw all over.

Binny recently returned from living in awesome Hong Kong and now works happily on beautiful Sydney harbour with other lovely creative folks, drinking copious amounts of dandelion tea, and is inspired by Jasper her rescue cat.

If you enjoyed this adventure, you might also like . . .